ƏN

One day, Mini was on her
way home from Grandma and
Grandpa's, when suddenly—

Screech!!

"Mini, look, it's a dog," her mom said. "And it's wearing shoes."

"Doggy?!!!!!" cried Mini.

SANGMI KO

A Dog wearing shoes

schwartz & wade books · new york

"Here, puppy!" Mini's mom called,
and the dog pranced right over.

"SO cute!" Mini shouted. "Can we keep
him? Please-oh-please-oh-please?"

Mini's mom looked everywhere for the dog's owner.
"This little fellow must be lost," she said at last. "We'll
have to take him home for now."

Mini was so excited!

She sang a song,

took the dog's shoes off
and put them back on,

bonked their heads together,

and took a nap with him.

At home, Mini wanted to keep playing.
The dog wasn't in the mood.

And then he started barking.

And barking.

"Mini, I think he's missing his family," said her mom.

"He's my family now. I found him."

"He's crying."

"He isn't crying! He's singing."

"His owner must be looking for him."

"But he has no dog collar! He doesn't belong to anybody."

"He has shoes," said her mom. "He belongs to someone."

"Maybe he just needs a walk," said Mini quickly.

"Let's go!"

Mini and her mother
bought a dog collar and leash

and went straight to the park.

There were dogs everywhere!

Soon Mini's dog had attracted quite a crowd.

"And friendly!"

"How adorable!"

"Look at those little shoes!"

"Sit!" "Beg!" "Paw!"

"And he's so smart!"

"Other paw!"

"Lie down!"

"Play dead!"

Mini was very proud.

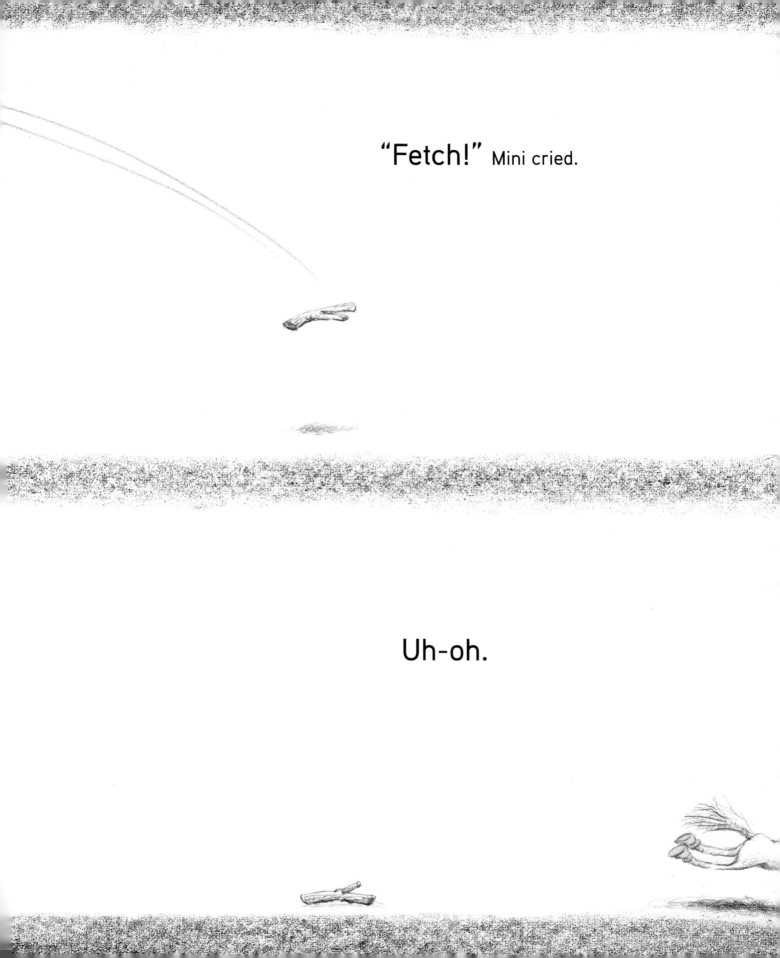

"Fetch!" Mini cried.

Uh-oh.

Mini looked everywhere—

inside the park

and outside the park.
But all she could find was a shoe.
"That's a dog that likes to run," said Mini's mom.

"Where are you, doggy?" cried Mini.

The next day Mini's mom took her to the shelter to try to find the dog.

"Doggy!"

Mini sat down and
gave the dog a big hug.

Then she took him home.

Now Mini knew that someone
else must be missing the dog too.

It didn't take long for his owner to show up.

A few days later, Mini and her mom knew just where to go . . .

. . . to find a dog of Mini's very own.

For those who were there—my family,
my sister's family, and doggies Malti,
Ray, and White

How to Adopt a Dog

• You must be at least 18 years old to adopt a dog from a
shelter, so kids need help from a parent.

• Do some research online to prepare yourself for the
responsibilities of pet ownership and make sure you
can afford the cost.

• Find a shelter. Staffers can help choose the right dog for
your family.

• Be prepared to visit a shelter more than once to get to know
a potential adoptee. Make sure all family members have a chance to meet the
dog, and if you already have a pet at home, consider bringing him or her to the shelter, too.

• On the big day, bring a government-issued photo ID and proof of address; the name of a personal
reference, reachable by phone; and the adoption fee, which can range from $75 to $200.
And be sure to follow the shelter's advice about follow-up veterinary care, licenses, and IDs.

For More Information, Check Out These Websites

aspca.org

humanesociety.org

petfinder.com

Copyright © 2015 by Sangmi Ko
All rights reserved. Published in the United States by
Schwartz & Wade Books, an imprint of Random House
Children's Books, a division of Random House LLC,
a Penguin Random House Company, New York.
Schwartz & Wade Books and the colophon are
trademarks of Random House LLC.
Visit us on the Web! randomhousekids.com
Educators and librarians, for a variety of teaching tools,
visit us at RHTeachersLibrarians.com
The text of this book is set in AauxPro.
The illustrations were rendered in pencil and colored digitally.

Library of Congress Cataloging-in-Publication Data
Ko, Sangmi.
A dog wearing shoes / Sangmi Ko. — First edition.
pages cm
Summary: Mini finds a dog in the park wearing shoes but no
collar and begs to keep him, but soon she realizes that whoever
put the shoes on him loves the dog, as well.
ISBN 978-0-385-38396-7 (hc)
ISBN 978-0-385-38397-4 (glb)
ISBN 978-0-385-38398-1 (ebk)
[1. Dogs—Fiction. 2. Lost and found possessions—Fiction.] I. Title.
PZ7.K7875Dog 2015   [E]—dc23   2014010934
MANUFACTURED IN CHINA
2 4 6 8 10 9 7 5 3 1
First Edition